Product

Mark Ravenhill

Copyright © 2005, 2006, 2015 by Mark Ravenhill
All Rights Reserved

PRODUCT is fully protected under the copyright laws of the United States of America, the British Commonwealth, including Canada, and all other countries of the Copyright Union. All rights, including professional and amateur stage productions, recitation, lecturing, public reading, motion picture, radio broadcasting, television and the rights of translation into foreign languages are strictly reserved.

ISBN 978-0-573-70445-1

www.SamuelFrench.com
www.SamuelFrench-London.co.uk

FOR PRODUCTION ENQUIRIES

UNITED STATES AND CANADA

Info@SamuelFrench.com
1-866-598-8449

UNITED KINGDOM AND EUROPE

Plays@SamuelFrench-London.co.uk
020-7255-4302

Each title is subject to availability from Samuel French, depending upon country of performance. Please be aware that *PRODUCT* may not be licensed by Samuel French in your territory. Professional and amateur producers should contact the nearest Samuel French office or licensing partner to verify availability.

CAUTION: Professional and amateur producers are hereby warned that *PRODUCT* is subject to a licensing fee. Publication of this play(s) does not imply availability for performance. Both amateurs and professionals considering a production are strongly advised to apply to Samuel French before starting rehearsals, advertising, or booking a theatre. A licensing fee must be paid whether the title(s) is presented for charity or gain and whether or not admission is charged. Professional/Stock licensing fees are quoted upon application to Samuel French.

No one shall make any changes in this title(s) for the purpose of production. No part of this book may be reproduced, stored in a retrieval system, or transmitted in any form, by any means, now known or yet to be invented, including mechanical, electronic, photocopying, recording, videotaping, or otherwise, without the prior written permission of the publisher. No one shall upload this title(s), or part of this title(s), to any social media websites.

For all enquiries regarding motion picture, television, and other media rights, please contact Samuel French.

CHARACTER

JAMES – A film producer
OLIVIA – An actress

SETTING

An office

JAMES. So there's a knife.

And your eyes widen as you see the knife.

And he's pulled it out from under his…the knife comes out from…he's wearing a, a…robe

He's a tall fellow, a tall, dusky fellow and –

And now he uses the knife, he uses the knife and he slits open the plastic on his croissant and he puts the croissant in his mouth and he puts the knife in that sort of stringy pouch in front of him.

Now you want to call out, – you are just about to call out:

He's got a knife. The tall dusky fellow has got a knife.

But something – a decision, a small but important beat, you don't call out. You look down the aisle at the tanned and blonde and frankly effeminate airline staff and you don't call out.

Why? Why? Why? Well…

Let's just discover her shall we? Let's just discover Amy a beat at a time.

'Excuse me' you tells the dusky fellow 'that's my seat' – you've had the window seat since childhood and he stands to let you in and you open the overhead baggage container – your luggage is Gucci, Gucci are in, it's going to be fabulous, you opens the luggage container and…

There's a mat. A small oriental mat rolled up very neat.

Hold on your face. Surprise, apprehension, maybe, I just want you to…play it.

Is this yours?

Yes.

Do you do yoga?

No. That is my prayer mat. I pray.

Oh.

And you sit and you…you look out the window and you…fear…you're in an an aeroplane up in the air, next to a tall dusky fellow whose prayer mat is up above you and whose knife is in the pouch in front of you.

Ladies and gentlemen. Could I remind you to switch off all electrical goods?

And you reach into your bag and you takes out your mobile and you go to switch off your mobile phone and now we – close up on you – you look down at the mobile and something is triggered inside you, a chord of emotion resonates and we see – ah! Amy is wounded, there's a wound and it's something about the mobile, something about the…it's a narrative hook and it's empathy.

I know you're going to love her. I hope you're going to love her. She is three dimensional. And I'd love to see you play three dimensional again after those last three, four…

And now the fellow turns, he turns, the tall dusky, fellow he turns and suddenly his head is on the shoulder of your suit – it's Versace, Versace are on board, it's a Versace suit – his dusky head is on the fabulous shoulder of your fabulous Versace suit and he falls asleep.

And you look at, you look at him…you…his smell is so different.

And do you know what you want to do? Do you know what you want to do? Well I'll…

You want to…you actually want to…you want to reach out to the knife…reach out to the knife and you want to grab hold of the knife okay and pull the knife out of that stringy pouch and you want to feel the weight of the blade in your hand and then you want to thrust it into him, in and out and in and in and out and in out until there is blood, there is blood shooting from that dusky frame and the blood is shooting over you and you're more blood than face and you want to call out:

This is for the towers. This is for civilisation. This is for all of us you bastard.

You don't say that. You don't do that. That's an interior monologue. You play that? I want you play that with your eyes. Can you play that with your? Well of course you can, of course you can. I love your work.

This is for all of us you bastard.

You see? You see? Amy is wounded. She is…to each of us the wound, to each the wound is different. It sounds classical but it's me, it's my note to my writers…show me the wound…and…please…I will show you Amy's wound if you'll – yes? yes? yes?

It's a thrill to have you in the room.

So Amy doesn't touch the knife, she leaves the knife, the knife is untouched and the plane lands and the dusky fellow puts the knife under his robe and he takes his prayer mat from the baggage container and that should be…they should never meet again but…this is the world of the heart, this is the screen the dream, this is movie-land, so, so, so…

It's rainy night, a storm at Heathrow, a broken heel on your Jimmy Choos and the only taxi left and it's his taxi and suddenly he's saying:

Please – get in.

Fear but somehow excitement. The adventure has begun. Into the car of a stranger.

And you climb in with fear and excitement and there's the prayer mat and there's the knife on the seat between him and you and you:

Which way are you going?

I don't know. Which way you going?

I – I – I –

You gonna take me home?

Take him home? Take him home? Are you going to take him home?

Cut to your face. Cut to the knife. Cut to the prayer mat. Cut to his – and the lighting favours him now okay? Something in the lighting – for the first time he looks handsome.

And you, and you, and you – you play the, her aching sexuality. Which I know you…

Your sexuality aches and he's handsome and you ignore the prayer mat and the knife and you say to the the cabbie:

The docklands please.

And he says:

Docklands love course love.

And you exit east from Trafalgar Square.

You live in an abattoir, it's on old converted abattoir, that is now a massively cool loft style apartment and it feels good to be home and strange and exciting to be letting the dusky fellow into your world but you open the door and you let him in and he puts down the knife and the prayer mat on your floor and you offer him wine but he doesn't drink but you do drink –

And you're nervous and you drink the better part of a bottle and your eye occasionally flicks to the knife and the prayer mat and now you've drunk the bottle and you are…

'I'm Amy. I open call centres and call centres, I travel around and around and around in dwindling circles around this shrinking globe.'

A man, a tall, dusky man in your apartment.

Your sexuality is so…it's aching, it's aching…it's inflamed and you – you surprise yourself – but you want him, you want him, you want the dusky fellow and you and you press yourself upon him.

Mohammed.

But he's frightened. He's a virgin and he knows nothing of this world of aching sexuality and he's frightened.

Amy I'm frightened.

Mohammed don't be frightened. Don't be…ssshh. Ssssh. Ssssh.

And you lead him to the bed and it's very beautiful – and you have a body double, Beata is your body double – and you lead him to the bed and you slip his body from his robes and at last your ache can be, can be, can be…filled.

And he is slow and unsure and clumsy at first but then as you move together, body and heart and…as you find the music of your…and now you begin to come and come and come and come and come and it's the orgasm of your life.

To find yourself, to find yourself, you – Amy – with your wound, to find yourself so at one with this dusky fellow is so…strange. We have to…we have to see that in your face. Can you play that? Can you…? Of course. I love your work. I love it. I've seen you do those turns on a sixpence. Hate. Love. Click. Power. Subjection. Click. I've seen you do that with a shit script and a cast I wouldn't wish on a mini-series. You're fabulous and this is fab – it's gonna be fabulous once it's been punched up.

But then – time passes in the night – time passes in the night and maybe you fall asleep but you wake, you wake – a jolt – uh – and you reach out – you reach out – you reach out and – you're – like so many times before you're alone in the bed.

Has he –? Has he gone? Has he taken you and gone?

Your eyes adjust to the darkness. No. He hasn't gone. He hasn't…there is the prayer mat and there is the knife just where he left them on your floor so he hasn't gone he's just, he's…

And then you see him. You see his dusky frame. You see the dusky frame moving about your incredibly cool loft style apartment – which was once an abattoir – and you see him and he's moving about and he's looking at your white goods and he's looking your black goods and your chrome goods and your beech goods and your plasma and your blue tooth and your exercise equipment and you know, you know, you know what he's doing and you throw yourself, you throw your naked – Beata's naked body from the bed and the words just come up, they just come up from inside you and you scream:

Stop judging me. Stop fucking judging. So my life is worthless. So I'm busy but it means nothing. So all I have around me is clutter and no value. So I never had a belief. So I'm all alone and I'll let the first human being inside me who shows me the slightest.

So so so so.

(We had a theatre writer work on this bit.)

And you what about you? Who gives you your orders? The Imam? The Dictator? Allah? Oh open your eyes, open your eyes. What would you like to do to me eh? Given half a chance. Cover me up? Stone me. But you'd like to.

That's stopped him. That's stopped him in his tracks and he's just stopped and he's listening to you.

'How can you how dare you feel superior to me? I am freedom, I am progress, I am democracy – and you are fear and darkness and evil and I hate you.'

His sperm is still dribbling down your leg. That's a private note. We won't shoot it.

And now you, there are tears, you are, the tears come up and now – your wound – as if on impulse, a beat, fast beat, you reach for your mobile and you call up a message, a message from the past, a message from – the time when the wound began, when all the hurting began to hurt.

And you – message on conference and you place it there in the middle of the floor down by the prayer mat and down by the knife, and you place your mobile phone down and you stand naked and Mohammed stands naked – like Eve, like Eve – and you listen to:

Oh my god oh my god oh my god oh my god oh my god. (It can be punched up.)

Oh my god Amy something's got the tower. They've… the other tower is on fire.

And – Amy sweetheart I think they've got us too. I think they hit our tower sweetheart. We're on fire. Shit. We're on fire. And I'm gonna have to jump baby and I – I just want you to know Amy I love you, I love you, I love you with all my – aaaaah.

And the message ends and Amy falls, falls to the floor and sobs. Which I think you can, I know you can…

I get alot of scripts. It's my job. I get…there are hundreds of thousands of stories and they're sitting on my desk and mostly they are, they are, they are…

The effluent of the soul.

Nobody understands the basic, the truth the, wound.

But this script, this story, I – I have been touched, I have been moved by this –. When I – I have lain on the floor in my office and wept when i read this script you see? You see?

And I want to…

There are powers greater than me. There is a Higher Power. I cannot greenlight. And I have been to the Power and I have said: This is the one, this is the… I want to produce this script, I have wept like a woman at this script and now I must tell this story and the Power has said to me: Get someone big attached.

And so I – so I – so I – no bullshit – I thought of you. For Amy. You are my first, you are my only choice for Amy –

Because like her you are... I know you hurt, I know... it's there, it's up there on the screen, your raw wound for me, us all to see which is why you...

You fascinate and you excite me.

So let's...make a movie.

the message ends. The message from the past, the message from the towers and Amy falls to the floor of her fabulous apartment and she is sobbing and now she, she's calling out:

Troy's gone. I'll never see Troy again. Troy died in the towers and I'll never see Troy again.

And Mohammed comes to you and he puts his arms around you.

Ssssshhh.

And for a moment, there's comfort, comfort but then your POV on the knife and the prayer mat and you say:

Mohammed I have to know. I have to know Mohammed.

Sssshhh. Not now Amy.

Yes Mohammed I have to – are you Al Queda?

Not now Amy. Ssssh. sssssssh. Sssssh.

And he lies you down on the bed and he holds you and oh the comfort of that dusky frame.

Now let's not play Amy with any judgement please, no let's not judge...let's just...let's just play her as a woman as a woman who that night as she lay there fell in love, fell in love with a man, a man with a knife and a prayer mat, a woman who that night as she slept, as she slept in Mohammed's dusky arms, forgot, forgot for the first time since the 11th of the 9th of 2001, forgot the smoke and the confusion and the calls, and the droop and crumble of the towers, and she forgot the fall of Troy.

And let's – moment by moment, day by day – she is drawn into Mohammed's world, moment by moment, day by day, and other men begin to gather at her apartment, other men with their robes and their knives and their prayer mats – seven, then eight, then nine, then ten men at a time, their mats positioned on the floor, calling to Mecca, talking, planning.

Is this is a cell? Is this – a fundamentalist terrorist threat in the middle of your world?

You should ask, you should challenge but you're – it's love, you're in – wild, blind, stupid – and the Heart is a bigger organ than the Brain as we say in this business we call show.

And then one day they are there – Mohammed and the men are there with their knives and their prayer mats in your fabulous loft style apartment, and you're making their infusion and suddenly, the door opens, the door opens and you turn and you see, you see, you see, here, in your apartment, coming across your apartment, he's there in your apartment, in your apartment, Osama is in your apartment.

And he comes towards you and he smiles at you – it's a cruel smile – and he –

Bless you.

Why don't you –? there are knives, there are – why don't you attack? you could, you should, you –

It's inner conflict, you're experiencing, you're playing this inner conflict. Everything is – for the sake of Troy for revenge you should attack, you should revenge but you don't and you are kissed – you are kissed, a warm breathy kiss on the forehead from Osama.

And now the plan is revealed. Now the work of the cell is made known to you. Now you know that they are all evil men.

Europe is to be torn apart. The Hague. The Reichstag. Tate Modern. Suicide bombing. Each of these men is to be stuffed and strapped with explosives and then at midday tomorrow they will carry off buildings and people and nothing but misery and devastation will follow.

And now they're coming to Mohammed. To Mohammed's task. What will be Mohammed's task?

You want to cry out: 'no no no no Mohammed. I love you'. Your mouth is open but the words don't come.

And then you discover, then you learn, Osama turns, he turns and he gives Mohammed his mission: Disneyworld, Europe. He must blow up Disneyworld Europe.

And now you step forward and you hear yourself saying, as if another is speaking for you:

'I can't bear for you to do this Mohammed. I can't bear to lose you. I've already lost Troy. And I won't lose you. I'm a woman and I love this man.'

And then you turn to Osama.

'Let me go with him. Strap me and stuff me with explosives and let me go with him and let me die with my man in the middle of the day in the middle of the continent at Disneyworld Europe.'

'No woman can ever –'

'Please great Mullah please. I am a woman but I love this man and I want to die with this man.'

Minutes go by and we cut to the faces of the jihadists as they wait for the decision of Osama, their mullah. Cut to Mohammed – his eyes are misty. Cut to you – waiting, waiting.

And then Osama breathes and he smiles and he nods.

'Yes.'

You are to die with your man.

And that night you lie in Mohammed's arms, you lie and wait the call that will take you to the EuroStar and onto your mission, you lie in the dark and he says:

I love you Amy I love you all my heart and I thank Allah for your bravery to join me in suicide.

It's just something I have to do Mohammed.

But I fear. When my body is blown apart at the beat of twelve I will go to Paradise. It will be easy to leave this world and go to Paradise. Where will you go?

I... I... I... I...don't know Mohammed. Where there... can I come to Paradise?

No. You are not chosen for Paradise.

Oh.

These are our last hours together.

Then fuck me. Fuck me. Fuck me. Fuck me these last few hours. Fill me every way you can until I hurt and I just can't take you anymore. Come Mohammed come.

And he does and you are hungry, hungry, hungry but finally you're en-seam-ed bodies topple into slumber and then it comes, the nightmare comes

You are there, you are in Disneyworld Europe and you are stuffed and strapped with every explosive known to man and you look around – a minute to twelve and you look around – and you see the people and you can't see...these are good people, these are good, fat, happy, bright people. Queuing, eating, riding people. These are your people. What are you doing? What are you doing?

Forty seconds until you take them away. Forty seconds until you push your hand through all of us and rip it apart.

How can you do this? Why are you doing this?

'Aveu vous vu ma mère?'

You look down at the little girl with the ears and the balloon and she's what – three?

'Aveu vous vu ma mère? Je veux ma mère. S'il vous plait – je cherche ma mère.'

And you want to scream:

No fucking point sweetheart. No fucking point. She's a dead person. I'm a dead person. You're a dead person. We're all just dead people in the Magic Kingdom of Life.

But you don't – you take her hand – twenty seconds to go but you take her hand –

You you suicide jihadist you take the hand of the pretty little girl with her mouse ears and balloon and you begin to walk down main street because you think: better she has these last few seconds of comfort in the search for mamon than to die alone and in fear and despair.

The time is coming in now, it's coming – ten, nine, eight, seven, six –

The explosives on your body are pulsating and vibrating as if to will themselves to their deathly task –

Five.

Mama, mama, où est-tu mama?

Four.

A figure is approaching.

'Bonjour – J'm'appelle Mickey. Vous est ma amie. Comment t'appelle tu?'

I am Death. I am Death. Run Mickey. Run Magic Kingdom. I am Death.

Three.

'Bonjour – fille joli. Quelle balon jolie.'

'Ou est mama?'

Two.

'Je ne sais pas. Moi, je ne suis pas votre mère.'

One. Tiny beat – maybe it's not gonna, maybe it's not – maybe fate and computer error has saved the world but then –

Boom!

From your back and your chest and your sex the force comes, the explosive comes and in your last moment of your life that child's head, now ripped from it's body and the blood filling your eyes, that child's head is blown towards you and her voice fills your head as you die:

'Mamon.'

You wake with a start. It's three in the morning, three in the morning in your fabulous loft-style apartment and you look at Mohammed and suddenly you are filled with disgust.

What is this? What are you doing?

He shouldn't be here with you. He shouldn't be – he should be in an orange jump suit and he should be spat at and kicked and humiliated.

You pig. You dog. You worse than animal. Roll in this shit. Piss your pants. Eat your faeces cunt.

And you are resolved and you reach for the 'phone and you phone the special forces.

And you report everything – sometimes with tears, sometimes in anger – you tell the whole terrible tale.

And now van is on it's way to take… Mohammed and the explosives.

Alone again. Another man who turned out to be not right for you. Every year the hurt grows a little more, until one day it will be so raw you'll never love.

Just one last look, one last look at Mohammed before he goes.

He looks like a boy – who could have thought he would be…? – he looks like a boy.

And you move toward him and you sit on the bed and you run your fingers through his dark, dark hair.

I'm sorry Mohammed, I'm sorry.

And you lean forward and you kiss a gentle kiss upon the sleeping lips.

Bitch.

His eyes snap open, his hand is up and strikes across the jaw.

Bitch. Bitch. Bitch.

Ahhh!

Bitch. You have betrayed us.

His lithe body jumps from the bed and he kicks you in the stomach, there's no breath in your lungs, there's a gob of blood in your mouth.

You have betrayed Allah.

I won't do it. I won't kill innocent children.

And you fear for your life. You fear that Mohammed will kill you, dismembered corpse in your apartment and you remember Mohammed's knife. And something inside you says – get the knife – get the knife – it's lying there and he could use the fucking knife and slit me toe to crown. You rush for the knife, you hold it – and you look up. But he hasn't gone for the knife.

He's got a petrol can in his hand. Where did that come from?

He looks down at you. His eyes lock onto yours. The seconds pass. A lorry passes in the night carrying beef to Dover. (That's a detail).

And now there is sadness in his eyes and he says:

I am the weakness. I am the flaw. I was the lust that drove me to woman. I have betrayed jihad.

And he pours the petrol can over his dusky frame, shaking his hair like a girl in a shower after hockey.

This world is a place of suffering and unhappiness. Yes?

Yes. Yes. Yes.

Please Allah admit me to Paradise, please Allah. I failed Jihad but please Allah.

And now he moves to the aga and he picks up the matches and you see what he's going to do.

'Mohammed – don't.'

'But I have failed my mullah, I have failed my cause. Goodbye.'

He strikes the match.

'But Mohammed I love you I love you I love you with all my heart more than Troy more than the Towers your strength your mystery your heart I – Let's run away now, before the security forces, let's begin again, there's a cottage, the countryside –

No. I have loved you Amy. But we are just people. That's all there is. People. Lonely, wounded people and their loving hearts.

No. There is Destiny, there is Allah's will, there is the Cause. And all of these are bigger than people. I pity you my love in your small world of people. No purpose… How do you live with this? My sadness is with you.

He looks up.

Oh please Allah, let your servant come to Paradise.

And then – woosh – he's alight, the flame racing across his body and his skin and hair and crackling and the smell is almost sweet in your converted abattoir.

And then you – this feeling deep within and you call out:

Oh take me, take me Mohammed. Take me in those arms. I love you. I don't know you. I'll never know you.

I will never believe a thing you believe. But fold me in your burning arms, press your flaming chest against me, scorch me with your groin of fire.

Then as if in slow motion – fuck it, we are in slow motion – you run toward the burning man.

And now – a life avoiding, avoiding, afraid of death – character notes: your mother's cancer, your best friend's suicide, your father dwindling into Alzeheimered oblivion – all your life scared and your denial of death and now the freedom, the total exhilarating three dimensional freedom as you call on the Angel of Death to take you and

Yes Mohammed Yeeeeessss!

You're and you're closing in on him, you're reaching him, your hair is starting to crack and sizzle as the flames are inches from you and then, then, then, your arms enfold him and his skin begins to melt onto yours:

Yeeessssss!

And then there's the crack of glass – do you know Liz, fabulous little dyke gonna be doing ail your stunts? – the crack of glass as you both fall and fall and fall, four storeys and into the pool below.

Underwater those bodies, twisting around, the flames becoming smoke becoming charred and sodden, your bodies twisting one over the others.

Until you come up – eighty degree burns on his part, twenty degrees for you but

There's love, like a great wave of release suddenly there's love, there in the pool there's love and you kiss and caress and you fuck in the water, the pleasure of the lovemaking, the pain of the burns all rolling into one.

But then they're there. The feds, the cops, the special ops – all the special forces of the world – and they pull Mohammed from your arms and you're screaming:

Please I love him. You have to – love will conquer this. I know it. Yes there is terror and horror and he's done wickedness yes – but we've found love here tonight and I –

Your final vision. Your final vision of Mohammed – the body a mass of burns, the smell of chlorine, the feel of him still inside you – a vision as the butt of a gun pushes you to the ground and the doors of the van open, the savage barking of a dog, the manacles clipping around the hands and feet of this man you love.

You rush into the street – you throw yourself into the path of the van – you are on the verge of madness now – I'd love to see you play the verge of madness – you block the path of the van – surely they must stop for you? – but the van is racing toward you – at the iast moment your nerve cracks and – wham! – you throw yourself out of the way.

Your cowardice. How you despise your cowardice. When an eighteen year old boy can blow himself up why can't you stand in front of a racing vehicle to save the man you love?

You pick yourself up from the pavement with difficulty. Already the bruising is beginning. You see the TV crew, the redhead with the microphone running towards you in the night and you're very wet and very cold and very alone.

No. He isn't a bad man, you tell the News. He is a good man and I love him.

And then your stomach loops, your knees disappear and you lose consciousness.

You're out for a couple of days. Your Mother cares for you. Your mother or a neighbour or an aunt or blah blah blah. She's a mentor okay? Too old to fuck, too old to kick-ass but we have a place for her in our world.

And this wise old woman, this woman whose sexuality has died so that she might think of higher things, this woman says:

Hush now child hush. You must forget him. You must let Mohammed go. There is a time for everything and your time for Mohammed has ended and now is the time to live a new life.

And you look up from the bed and you feel the warmth of her wisdom and you say:

Yes MotherAuntNeighbour yes.

And so there is an emptiness. An emptiness which once he filled. And your life begins again. You begin to spin around the globe again. There's the constant drive drive drive to outsource customer relations to expanding economies. There are several weeks in China.

And back at home Nathan gets in touch again. Nathan who loved you at school. Nathan who married the fitness instructor but lost her in the railcrash. Nathan who has loved you all the time.

And you sit in sushi bars and theatres and taxis with Nathan and he holds your hand and he touches your knee and all the time he's telling you what a special person you are but really there is nothing that you hear.

And you take Nathan in your mouth. You take his broad beautiful cock in your mouth and you force it back and back into you so that you gag because when you gag you know you'll feel something. But you don't feel anything.

And you plead with Nathan to hit you about the head. You put the club in his hand and say: Come on come on strike me. But he loves you in such a tender way and he runs into the night and that's Nathan gone.

You hang about the coach station and you pull up your skirt for teenagers in toilets and in alleyways – looking for a smell that will drown the scent of Mohammed.

(This is edgy okay? This is fucking – fucking edgy stuff okay? What do you think? What are you thinking? I'd love a word here. Just a word to let me know how I'm…

I'm pitching my bollocks off and that –

I like it. I like it. Enjoy your power. I would. If I had that power then I would use it.

You bitch you bitch. I love you, you bitch. Respect to the bitch.

No stay stay stay. Stay. Hear the end of the story. Hear the end of the story or I'll…

Thank you.)

It's a bar. A bar with a TV screen. A fucking scuzzy prostitutes and drunkards bar by the coach station when you first see the images of Mohammed on the TV screen. They've been smuggled out of the off-shore prison. It's a blurry image – nothing more than a grey shadow moving across the TV screen. But you know straight away. You know the man you love as he is dragged across the screen, the hair torn from his scalp. And you see her apply the electrodes to his testicles, you see the dignity in his face as the other guards laugh and jeer, you see the spit on his face, then his body dancing as the electrodes burn at the testes you have held so often in the night.

You sit in your fabulous loftstyle apartment that evening and you watch that image played over as it rolls through the news and you listen to the experts and the politicians and the lawyers and the celebrities trying to give it their story, every time a new story as once again the electrodes are clipped onto

Mohammed's sac, as the spit hits his face, the jeers and the jaunts and then the electricity dancing through his body.

And, just as suddenly as the power joits through your lover, the resolve jolts through you. You leap from your chair, you throw your towel to the ground and you turn your naked body to the screen and you call out:

Hold on. Hold on. Because I'm coming, I'm coming to save you – lover.

And we crane crane, crane as though the gods, the heavens, the eternal powers hear and endorse your cry.

A montage. You're training. A boy's boxing club in the east of the city where you push yourself until your eyes swell with blood. The icy lake where you swim for hours before even the ducks are awake. The Tibetan monastery where you learn to breathe and kick and chop. The mountain state where your Kalashnikov is slung across your breast ready to fire as the targets go flying into the sky.

And as one image melts to another, we see Amy disappearing from view. She's gone. Amy – who once lived on coffee and air-miles and longing – Amy – who never found the perfect diet, never found the perfect man, never found a therapist she could trust – this Amy is ripped away to reveal a creature of muscle and will and strength.

You are hero. Before you we are nothing. Before you we – oh saviour, oh saviour, oh saviour.

If only you would save me, if only – this story were… there is an inner truth to this st…but…it's what we would want to…

No. You're right. Fucking pointless. I'm fucking pointless. What is this piece of crap? What is this…? What is this story? What's this…three mill on an opening weekend? What is that? It's shit.

So you don't…have to…

I'll call a car…

(*to phone*) A car for…yeah, yeah…account.

Thank you.

Listen just…

Let's just end this…okay?

That final night in your fabulous loftstyle apartment that was once an abbatoir. And in your fabulous apartment you take Mohammed's mat from the floor and you bless it and you place the mat in your rucksack and you take Mohammed's knife and you kiss the blade and you slip the knife amongst the weapons that are slung about your waist.

And then we cut to –

Boom! The explosion crashes open the door to the corridor and in you come – a fury in fatigues.

'Where is he? Where is he?' you scream at the Cuban guard pushing him against the wall. 'Where the fuck is he?'

And your fist – crack crack crack – against the Cuban's skull.

'I'm coming to fucking find you' you scream, blasting at the guards who come running toward you. Your bullets tear into them and hurtle them against the walls and the blood begins to run in rivers down the corridors of Uncle Sam's detention centre.'

'Mohammed! Mohammed! Mohammed!'

Boom! You blow open the doors to the first cell and out they come the men and women in their orange jumpsuits, blinking into the light and calling to Allah as they dance with their liberty.

But he's not there. So many faces – but not the face of the man you love.

You blow open the second door, the third door, the fourth door – and they are pouring down the corridors of the prison now, a great carnival of the enchained.

There he is! Mohammed! You run towards him, you throw yourself towards him, you pull at his shoulder –

'Please?'

The stranger is terrified at this fierce warrior who is clinging to him.

So. The search goes on and you go into the lift and down and down and down – until…

The light is dim here. Many floors above the orange jump suits and the guards are fighting but here there's not a sound. 'Pad like the cat, strike like the tiger', said the Tibetan monk and so you pad through the dimness – and strike like the tiger as the guard turns the corner, slitting his throat with one keen slice from Mohammed's blade.

And finally the silhouette against the bars. And he's weeping.

'Oh Mohammed.'

The hair has been pulled from his skull, he's burnt, he's bruised and – 'Amy?'

'Yes Mohammed.'

'Go. I won't see you.'

'Please –'

'Western bitch who destroyed my bond to Allah.'

'Mohammed.'

'Western bitch who defiled my body and tore at my heart.'

'Mohammed.'

'Western bitch who cannot see Paradise.'

'Please Mohammed. I have been…there was Amy and I spit on her. I spit on her restless, pointless, aching decadence. Yes I spit. I spit – and I pray to be reborn – reborn in Allah's eye and I will not rest until this world is purged of the infidel and all stand pure before Allah – together we will do this my love we will fight and struggle and work until this hollow world is purified and all are ready for paradise.'

'This is prison is hell.'

'And I have come to take you back. Please Mohammed let me…'

'Yes my love.'

And so you blast open the bars and out he steps, the broken figure of this man you love. And how gently you hold him in that moment. And how tender but how lingering is that kiss as your souls melt into one.

(There will be awards for this, there will be prizes – but let's not sully…)

'Come' you tell Mohammed and you lead him down the corridor but –

Tuh! The lone guard – you take her out but not before her bullet ricochets around the walls and – slow, slow, slow motion drills its way into Mohammed's head. He crumples – slow – and – slow – the blood stutters from his mouth and ears.

There is no God, no Angels, no nothing in our world but still…

There is actually a moment. We're going to need a fantastic lighting-cameraman but there is actually ta moment when the soul leaves the body. Have you ever…? I've seen it. I've seen it and – erm – if we can get that on celluloid then…they can fucking kiss my arse.

So Mohammed's soul leaves his body for Paradise.

And you mourn him and you mature in that moment – not in a gradual – bereavement matures you in a moment

And you see it's all screens and show and display and symbols and acting make believe emptiness.

And you pull out the knife and you feel the weight of the knife in your hand and the sharpness of the blade and you turn the blade toward you, oh to do it, to do it, to do it, just to feel the dignity of Ancient Rome –

But then –

Cut to your POV.

And it's the rucksack with the prayer mat.

And you take out the prayer mat. And you play: The knife or the prayer mat? Prayer mat or the knife. Which will it be? Which will you…?

Knife. Prayer Mat. Face. Knife. Prayer Mat. Face.

And then…you put down the knife. You don't kill yourself.

And you move across the floor and you reach the prayer mat and you look around – unsure which way to position yourself – but then –

A sudden swell of certainty – you're underscored – and then you kneel down, you kneel down upon the mat and – she's a great character:

Allah? I will revenge, Allah.

Thank you for listening. Thank you for coming here. It's been a privilege to tell the story. And you if you want to go back to your you know manager and agent and PR and your people and you know take the piss, use the script to…then fine, fine, because at least I've told you, I have told you.

 (Exit **OLIVIA**. **JAMES** *phones:)*

Hey! Loved it. Loved it. She loved it.